MURDER IN DARK AFRICA

Agibu the Cursed Prince:

A DIVINE SOLUTION

by

Catherine Ashford

Gritt & Witt Publishing

Other Titles from this Author

Non-Fiction

A Book of Hope and Inspiration:

If Only You Could Tell - **By Penny Hall.**

I Cried: I Know Why I did, The Woman That I Am - **By Selina Scott.**

ABC With a Difference: **By Selina Scott.**

The Healing Love- - An Infectious Thing - **By Catherine Ashford.**

The Other side of Polygamy: My Perspective, Is it a Curse or a Cult? - **By Selina Scott.**

Unveiling Hidden Riches - The Truth, Be Bold and Make it Happen - **By Penny Hall**.

Voice of Reasoning: My Better Education - **By Catherine Ashford**

Understanding Life's Secret – The Will Concept **by Catherine Ashford**

Fiction

A Horn in The Ground and Other Stories.

Stories From Afar

Bessy and the Moonshine Baby –

The Midnight Visitor of Culture and Other Stories

The Curse Goes On

I0567802

Published in UK BY Gritt & Witt

ISBN: 978-1-874550-43-3   PRICE:£6.99

Acknowledgement

Thank you to my father, who tells so many folk tales to us when we were younger. At some point the stories gets so frightening, and it becomes difficult for us to sleep.

My father, he was a great storyteller in life. His own father was an herbalist, and will go into to the bush to find healing plants. It is from this, that would bring about his stories that he will tell my father. Now my father tells us about his father's encounter with strange beasts, and dark things. So, we were hearing dark stories from ancient of times. Now, I tend to lighten the dark side to brighten the tales. My stories are not dark; but has a tiny twist taken from my father's generous story telling gifts to his children.

He could be telling us stories, and we would be dozing. He would then say, 'Mr. eye is coming for his eyes. I can see him going with them.' At that point we would wake up. Then he would joke and said, 'good job, you catch him quickly, because if he got your eyes, you would not have any, as he would take them with him.' It was funny and frightening at the same time. We would all start laughing, and at the same time struggling to keep our eyes open. He was a genius in making us happy. He was so good at

storytelling, that he would always be making jokes on the go. He was a real dad or father to us all. He finds time to do things with us. He encouraged all of us to excel, and many of the tales he told to us, I have developed further and incorporate them into my writings. At this point, I want to show gratitude, and appreciation to him; and say, thank you PaPa, you are sorely missed. In his loving Memory.

Dedication

Extra-ordinary Story,

This book is dedicated to the people of a small village in Africa. To those who like telling stories and fables. Those who taught us about making time worth living. Also, my precious father who likes telling us Anansi Stories,

Let us also remember the youths in prayers. Also, the young men who are killed in senseless attacks all around the world; and wherever they may be. Let us pray for those that are growing up in a society that is so violent, loveless, and difficult to live in. Upon all these killings it appears that we are powerless, and can do nothing.

Disclaimer

This is a fiction, but it depicts a story that many would be familiar with. Any names, places of form of culture used in this book is fiction. If in case it appears to relate to anyone reading this book or person or people, or place that you know, it is purely accidental. It has nothing to do with any real person or places that exist in this world.

Quote

The simple things in life we all take

for granted. But God uses the

foolish things to his glory.

Contents

The Curse Goes On

MURDER IN DARK
AFRICA AND
THE CURSED PRINCE

A DIVINE SOLUTION!

By

Catherine Ashford

The Curse Goes On

Introduction

I am delighted to have the opportunity to write this story. It is something that has impact in everybody's lives and everyone. It does not matter where you are living. It deals with issues affecting so many people in society. The world now, is horrible. There is evil, there is violence, it is scary, and it is horrible, and it is a dangerous fact. How can we all help to prevent violent crimes such as knives and guns? How can we change the now, and the future of crimes in our society? These are all facts, and it is crystal clear, with crimes increasingly visible everywhere in the world.

I expect everyone to do more to deal with this crime. This is one world, and one people. Let us show love to everyone, regardless state, culture, class, race sex or the young, youth, adult, and ageing people. We should be a society who cares for all and for everyone regardless. ....

Chapter 1

A Prince was Born

Once upon a time, there was a day when no one wanted to bother about anything. Why was that? That day was special, so special for all; and indeed, it was one that would be celebrated by the whole village for years to come. It happened during the month of the raining season. It was cold, and no sun was showing up, and the people looked a bit anxious. People were terribly busy moving up and down doing their own things. There were people standing around talking. Everybody wants to know what the excitements was all about. Then the time came when the announcement was made. Could you believe; it took so long for the people to know about the big news? It was a huge news for them.

This was the story of the birth of the Chief's long-awaited son. The announcement came, and it was a boy. This was the first celebration for a long time that had happened in the Chief's house, not since the day he married Fatima. The Chief was waiting for an heir to his throne. There were whispers everywhere that the Chief had no heir born to him, and everyone knew that he would be the only heir as none of the other wives had any boy child. There was great celebration, and there was going to be a future worth looking forward to for the Chief. Fatima was married to the Chief for the purpose of bearing an heir. Time has gone out for the three other wives and the Chief was getting on in life too.

When the child was born, he became an incredibly special person in the Chief's household. That meant so much to Pa Amadu (the Chief)…….. On that day, came the long-awaited arrival of his son. He was a child that was to be exceptional in the family.

Everyone would have to know about him. People would have to deliver tender, and loving care to this sweet little person; born to a very wealthy family. His arrival would be beyond comparison to any child born in the village, nor the celebration would be compared to anyone done in the village. So, it would be one of that kind that anybody had known before.

Pa Amadu, as they call him. He is the people's elder, and the head chief of the Village. In that chiefdom, all older person, or people in powerful position, earns the title of 'PA,' and a woman will be known as 'Mammy,' so as to show clear boundary, and respect for the senior members in society.

The Elders

With those titles comes knowledge of so many things. They are qualified to teach the young people; and also, to keep the society together. Part of their duty is to sit in native courts to judge disputes, and cases that are brought before them.

These are the people who organise celebrations, such as crowning of chiefs, weddings, and christenings. They are responsible to gather the community together. To distribute lands that are bought, and encourage the men into farming, and the women into trade for life sustenance. The girls are taught to cook, and to conduct domestic at home, and the boys helps in the farm with the herds of the family.

The family of Pa Amadu

His wife Fatima had gone through her ninth months of pregnancy with ease. It was the second week of the tenth month that Fatima had a brief pain. It was not that easy, as I flippantly said it. It was her first pregnancy.

Nevertheless, for her, it was like having pains for an entire year. Though it was short, and sharp, she was a strong woman, being that she was young. Then it happened so quickly, that everyone thought, 'What a lucky way of having a baby.' This says it all, that the baby was excited, and ready to come into this world. You would think it feels like a blink of an eye, yes, but there is a new baby in the world. He was going to do exploits. Though it did not feel like that, only history will explain the rest.

The child Fatima's husband wanted had finally entered the world – It was a baby boy. She was excited, he was excited; and everyone was excited.

Pa Amadu (The Chief), the father of the child decided on the name 'AGIBU.'

Fatima agreed, because she liked the name very much.

They were ignorant of the facts of the circumstances that surrounded the name of Agibu. There was a curse associated with it. Who would have thought that a name could have had a hidden implication? No, not everyone is accustomed to names with blessing, and names with curse.

The child was handsome, perfectly made with every parts well built. Ten toes, ten fingers, two eyes, two ears, a mouth, and a nose. All perfectly, and physically made.

The Naming Ceremony of the Prince

In their religious culture, a 'Naming Ceremony' was of significant importance. It is huge. For as much as we know, an heir is born, and it is something to be proud of, and to show case to the community at large. This celebration requires everyone to dress up.

The people, Men as well as women, will dress in their national wear; and the women's head gear which becomes the most elaborate head wear showcase in the celebration. Each one represents the tribe that they came from. Anyone can think of what this celebration would look like by just seeing the elaborate dressing parade. Oh, there is a uniform, the people call it Ashobi. This is chosen by the Chief's wife, and in this case, it is Fatima. Also, the Chief's clan would choose their own dress code. It is an elaborate celebration. A parade was to be staged for that matter.

At the ceremony, the elders of the town were to be invited. As everyone would expect, they too would go with the law of the Chief's compound, and policy of dressing for any occasion that he calls. There is a different dress code for every occasion. Just name it. The birth of the child, the naming ceremony, the engagement ceremony, the eve of the wedding ceremony, and also the wedding day.

At last, there is a tone down of the dressing when it comes to funerals. However, there were always uniform dress code. Depending on the status of the deceased person. So, celebration is a huge business in this country.

The people of that town knew the family very well for their enormous wealth and generosity. It was going to be a grandiose thing, as they usually do in all of their celebrations. In the Chief's house there would always be food to eat and drink. Sometimes the poor would always be in standby to go for handouts.

In fact, Pa Amadu as the people of his village called him was a business mogul and a Chief.

Therefore, at the ceremony, the people came with their baggage full of gifts. The visitors entered the room where the baby was laid, one after the other. Those who attended came with their blessings, and others with evil in their eyes. On their way out, few of them made predictions to the parents about their child's future.

This had been going on for thousands of years, even from previous generations to generations.

The simple things in life we all take for granted, can also become a huge thing in other people's lives. But God uses the foolish things to his glory. So, therefore this story became one of the foolish to be made wise in this kingdom.

One of the elders, a man of the ceremony would have blessed the Ceremonial things, such as: water, bread, kola nut which is placed on top of a powdered white rice, made into dough. Cooked and uncooked doughs.

The Kola Nuts

There would be incantations and prayers. On the arrival of the guests, they would be offered kola nuts and water, a piece of the uncooked rice dough. Made with sugar, and another one with salt. The Kola nuts will be placed on top of the rice on a white plate.

This is usual in most African homes.

The kola nuts symbolize hospitality respect and friendship. In an African home, it is a customary tradition for the host to serve kola nuts and water to their visitors.

The Kola Nut is used in African ceremonies, such as weddings, funerals, naming of baby ceremonies, funerals, visiting graves, and also used as health benefits. Officially, the Kola nut is a ceremonial thing used in the people's everyday lives.

Kola nut is amongst the gifts brought to pledge loyalty to a woman's family when a man goes to ask her hand in marriage. When the family of a man goes to pledge to marry a woman, the term 'Put Kola' is used.

The kola nut is a huge thing in the African people's lives. It is meaningful, without a kola there is no marriage agreement. This is because it represents part of the dowry in the form of money.

At the ceremony, the kola nut ritual was ready to be made. All the guests had arrived in their fabulous attire, and everybody were sitting outside under a massive Baffa. (a tent like covering)

No one knew what the elders would say about this baby. It was the first child of both Fatima and her husband Pa Amadu who has three other wives and had other children with them, to be exact six children, and all were girls, so they were ecstatic.

Pa Amadu gave the name written in a paper and gave to the elder to be read out. Fatima was standing beside him. The name was written in their Religious Alphabet.

After the name was read, it was noticeable that one Elder member in the house, was seen to move his head from side to side. It was as though he was in disapproval of the name. The Elder had thought the name was not suitable at the time of the birth of this precious child.

'AGIBU' (The name Agibu came with a curse, and hard luck in life, if used during that time of the season.) One member spoke softly and quietly.

An Elder got up, walked towards the religious leader, and spoke in a soft voice in his ears. All he was saying was that the name had a curse; and they should not name the child with it.

The chief does not know this. However, no one is prepared to say anything. The leader who knew what this meant, thought it was a good idea, that the parents should choose another name to avoid the curse of the name AGIBU.

So, no one was talking, but it was time to do the ritual with the kola nuts. The leader took the nuts eight in total as the child was a boy. It was broken up into twos, then they would chant spiritual words throw them on the floor; and read the meaning of how the kola nuts were turned, whether inside or outside up.

The leader will interpret what the meaning is. It would either be a blessing, prosperity or could be ill-fated future for the child. This ceremony with kola nut is sacred, and the people rely upon it to prophesy for them.

Elder Karim stopped the naming ceremony, and called both parents to one side of the room after hearing what the leader had said.

He wanted to explain what he heard and the belief of the community so, he spoke to them. He explained the curse placed on the name at the time of the child's birth. Pa Amadu, and Fatima were adamant; and would obviously not giving in to the elder's advice, about woe on the child.

They both thought that there was nothing to it. It was nothing, and no big deal. It was all to do with superstition.

Chapter 2

The Cursed Name Agibu

It was known that such a curse would happen once in every hundred years. An old woman cursed the last person known to have had that name, more than a hundred years ago. The curse had never been cancelled. No one knew how to do it. The gods they bow to cannot change anything. So, the curse continued and goes on.

People just let it go on. Instead, they stopped using the name Agibu to name their children. A bit like the Jacob story, or Jabez (1 Chronicles 9-10), not exactly, but rather similar to naming children with names that have negative impact.

This was an unfortunate happening explained here:

The Attack

A boy called Agibu attacked an old lady aged one hundred years. He mugged, beat her, and left her for dead on the ground.

The woman in her pain, put a curse on the day her attacker Agibu was born. 'Let curse befall all who bears that name in every hundred years.' Said the woman before she died.

Agibu who attacked this old woman, died a very gruesome death at the age of twenty-nine years. He was never to live for a day after the date of his twenty-ninth birthday. Nothing ever on this earth could avert the curse. If only they knew that there is just one information to help break that curse, tragedy would never happen. But no one knows that, and none is willing to research a way to get rid of this terrible situation. All the elders could do is mark it down in their book of truth, that the name should not be used on particular time of year. So, 'the Curse Goes On.'

The elders knew this, and so, they recorded it in the books of truth. Fatima insisted that she liked that particular name. She insisted that the name stayed, and that she was sticking to it. Amadu had no choice; and because of the love for his wife, and peace in the home he agreed with her decision to keep the name.

The elder leader Pa Karim gathered everyone including the family of the baby. He made the proclamation Just before the Ceremony. After he had finished the proclamation, he went on with his explanations with regards to the name.

Then Pa Karim asked for silence, so that they could pray for them. He called to the people, and asked that everyone should keep the child, and the family in their prayers. To avert the curse. Elder Karim added that they should pray regularly for Agibu. Next, the elder continued to wrap up the naming ceremony in readiness for the party. A woman came and collected the kola nuts and break them into small pieces and shared to everybody.

The party was enjoyable. There would always be food to eat and drink. They danced and sang, meaningful songs relating to the naming ceremony. People introducing each other to those they have not met before. Telling of all what they knew that is going on in the town. Especially, violence by youth and rogues.

This is the town riddled with poverty, with half naked children that roam the streets. They are idle. No school or proper sanitation in the home nor in the streets. The scene is that of shanti town. The rain appears to come in its season which allows the street's open gutters to overflow, at all times, dragging the rubbish, and debris around with its gushing stream. No proper drainage to help with the rain floods. Their homes are flooded. The mud houses and the corrugated sheets managed their living lifestyle. They are poor. With no running water, the children managed to collect from the stream; as well as the rain that made it possible for the children to catch water dripping down from the corrugated roofing sheet. They would often play and dance under the rain, running around, and playing catch me if you can. But they are difficult to catch with no clothing on as their bodies are slippery and wet. It was always fun for them, and they would be excited. Singing, 'raindrops are beautiful, we run, play, and dance. Catch me if you can.' The children loved it when it rains. There is no school for them. They are a bunch of little unfortunate children. The ministry of health that is responsible for sanitation in that part of the town, is blind sided as the officials do not live in that community area. The children grew up and knew nothing but theft and crime. They usually graduate from petty street crimes to serious crimes of home burglary or even murder. The situation is pretty serious.

Imagine, one boy saying, 'this is where I get money to take to my family.' One cannot help but stand and watch whilst they are rummaging around fields of dirt, where flies, mouse, and other crawlies made their home. They find food, and things in the rubbish bags. They searched for things that can be sold for money. There are children who are responsible for feeding their family. Due to the civil wars that had left them disabled and poorer, than they were before any war even started. Everyone would see the people become refugees, and were running away into the city because they cannot farm. This was a serious matter when there is war going on, who can do farming? The people were frightened for their lives. As they may be killed or even take them as slaves. So, everyone was on fright mode.

At the naming ceremony, everyone enjoyed themselves. They had food to eat and drink. When the people left, they took food and drinks home too. The people used this type of ceremony gathering, as a meaningful networking, and it worked for them. It was a beautiful sight. After everyone had eaten and drank, it was coming to the end of the party. Speeches were made with encouraging words of blessings, including prayers said for the families.

However, no one knows who, and where or from whom are they asking these blessings. At the end of the day, it was a beautiful celebration. The multitude that was at the ceremony all were well fed enough, as well as to carry food away. Food to feed them and their family for a whole week, it was such a grand occasion. This was why the people were happy to spend money in buying the family clothes, to dress up; and show up in these types of occasions, because they knew it will be grand.

There will be food to eat, drink, and share. When the people came, they brought with them their own bowls, and bags with them when attending; so as to carry when they are leaving. So, the people knew there would be leftovers.

They shared food to the poor standing out at the gate, though they were not invited, they showed up anyway; but were not allowed in as they were not wearing the uniform, as family clothing (Ashobi). All the more it makes good reason, and the importance of buying the uniform to show that you were invited. Their animals were fed too.

Overall, it was a very, very, very grand, and beautiful occasion. Everyone was happy as they left the celebration.

'Agibu' the name that sealed the fate of the child - will the child die on his twenty-ninth birthday? So, the naming ceremony ended. Everyone left and went to their homes.

Elder Karim, by the end of the celebration, and before everyone left, he once more, explained to the people about the name of the child. The people came to the occasion in hundreds. But those people who knew about the effect of the curse were sad.

There are secret tears, but not everyone knew about the impact a name would cause to the family or any family for that matter. Nevertheless, others said prayers. I do not know who they were praying to, but they prayed before everyone dispersed.

Though there were those who could not figure out the reason for the sadness, but acknowledged that something was not right. No one did figure out whether it was for joy, fear or just for the sake of the solemn speech made. There were mixed feelings. People saw that the party was over, and it was now time to find their way back to their respective homes.

It was like everything was coming together as the attendees began to leave one by one, just as they came in. Could Agibu, die on his twenty-ninth birthday? I wonder, what will stop the 'Curse?'

Everyone knew about Agibu's situation. He grew up so fast, as if time were rushing him to get to where he should be. But the chief, Pa Amadu wanted an heir; and also want him to marry.

AGIBU'S YOUTH DAYS

There were discussions and meetings for the young prince's future. So, they started making plans to look for a suitable woman for him to marry. A virgin girl should be the suited woman to carry his grandchildren.

All the people in that small town knew the family, and about the situation. So, they talked and shared everybody's information. It is a small village where everyone knew each other very, very, well, and so they personally loved him too. Therefore, his story went around so fast before you could say, hello!

His parents educated him in the best school that was available to them in the town.

He was a very clever boy. In every class he sat, he had double promotions skipping one and on to the next one, and the next; and the next until he finished at an incredibly young age. He came top of the class all the time. He was a clever boy. His attitude, his behaviour, mannerisms were as perfect, as anyone would want it to be. In each month, his end of month class report is exemplary.

Agibu got a scholarship at the end of his secondary education. He was bright, and smart. He entered a Law school, as he was interested in Law. He studied extremely hard, and took his first law exams on his twenty-first birthday and passed. His parents were happy.

That even overshadowed the issues at hand, and made them forget the trouble ahead. He was the youngest to sit that exam that year. This was how clever he was. His parents did not accept the scholarship instead asked that it should be given to a less fortunate child. They paid his fees right through his university studies. They were extraordinarily rich, and prosperous family.

Whenever guests were around, they would say, he was very clever for his age. Everyone was talking about his achievements. 'Let us face facts, the guy was very clever, and he was intelligent too.' They said to themselves. He actually was the first young man in the village at that time to enter Law School, and graduate at that age.

The people were surprised that the boy was very clever, as if it is an impossible fact, but it was the truth. However, they loved him even more. You would not believe, when I say that he was a true walking encyclopaedia, a dictionary, and a library, all put together in his young brain. His parents were still thinking of him settling down, and marry, especially Pa Amadu.

After that exam, he continued studying, and being an intern in a law firm. Working as an apprentice to a senior Barrister. He wanted to become a Prosecuting Barrister.

He was determined to do his best in his law career, and he wanted to be able to get to the bar at a noticeably early age. This young man was ignorant of his fate, and what life meant to him. He was also clueless about anything going on. Throughout his childhood, Madiu stood beside him as loyal as he could be. He was the only one who was a close friend in his life. As his parents would not allow him to fraternise with too many friends, and the boy grew up to be so conservative. Madiu visits him, but he does not visit Madiu. Socially, Agibu is always with his family. He grew up close to them. But unknown to him regarding the curse behind his name. On the overall look, the prince has an infectious laugh with a pleasant countenance, all the more he was loved.

No one has ever explained fully to him, nor anything that surrounded his birth, let alone the controversy that was created on the day of his naming ceremony.

Pa Amadu, the father of Agibu, was in fear for the worst, if he were to tell him the truth. He had already tried ways in keeping Agibu away from trouble, by restricting his social contact with people, including having friends outside of their home.

He tried so many ways of preventing problems that would lead to his early death. Yet, he would not find himself to explain to Agibu about the meaning of the name; nor why he became so overprotective.

Agibu was a sensible man, by then, he had grown to be very handsome, and respectful. He was so loved, and sweet that he did not know about why his family were so protective. He did not know about his problems, and his fate at birth, nor about the prophecy. However, such a story of how it would affect him in life was kept from him. In addition, he knew nothing about the change suggested during his naming ceremony. There were those who want to believe that he knew something about the curse but not everything.

Once he was old enough, to understand things better, his father told him about the tradition of his family. Agibu by then had grown up. So, he humbled himself as a child of moral standing. In as much as he was well grounded; when he finally heard what was spoken against the name that he was given - that anyone bearing that name should become a cursed child, he was baffled, horrified and a little angry, and so he wanted to know more of what was lingering over him.

So, his heart sunk, he carried his hands over his head, he walked in strides up and down the room, and began to weep. He wept in front of his family. He knelt down prayed, and asked if 'god' would have it changed for good. The prince managed to get his mind and head through the whole saga, and his mother Fatima's obsession with the name Agibu. Then there was the father, Pa Amadu, the Chief, constantly struggling in his bowing to his 'god,' a graven image, and hoping this will all go away. At one moment he felt temporarily paralysed at the whole fuss regarding the name.

Agibu had an experience

The prince walked away from everyone into his room, and screamed: 'is there any God that can hear me, let me hear you?' he then went silent for a moment.

Then he felt a great surge of warmth rushed through his body as he stood there, then he fell on the bed from the attack. He did not know it was the holy spirit. He had a peaceful rest.

His only desire was to do all things right, so that he could help the less fortunate in the city. When he woke, it was like a bad dream; and could not even remember what they had been talking about.

The chief (Pa Amadu) began to ask for mercy that his eyes may not see all the evil that would befall his beloved son.

The Chief then sent for all the elders, the heads in the village, the chiefs, the Imams, people great and small, the rich, the poor, the sorcerers to gather together in the largest room – known as the grand room in the house.

The gathering was to pray for the boy Agibu. Collective prayers in a community group are valued by the people when things are not working as they should. So, there were mixtures of faith people, who came from every denomination. Since the Prince was told, he has not stopped crying, nor did he eat well since that day.

Fatima has the duty to prepare special goat soup in which she would have added native herbs to help strengthen him, and get him going again. Remember, he is going to be a groom shortly as his marriage is still on the table for discussion. As she prepares the food, she would be saying, 'what have I done to this poor boy, I only meant well.' They had earlier called for a doctor to come, but the boy was inconsolable. At that point.

Amongst the people that came, there were groups sitting in circle holding hands, and praying together. Everyone was doing their own thing, to help. People standing in various areas holding little books that I presume prayers are written on.

The prince's friend Madiu was with him and few other people consoling him to be a strong man. He should be the young confident person that he is, and to take the information with a pinch of salt. He was not to make anything serious of the issue.

Sixty minutes later, Agibu had understood the whole situation and had spoken for the first time after he had the news. He brought is mind round to the thinking, and understanding of his friend including other comforters, that this is all just folklore, and would not materialise anyway.

So, whilst all the people came to pray and comfort Agibu and the family; there were hopes that so far nothing of such grave trouble will occur. Everybody was hopeful. Agibu does not look heavily distressed as he was earlier on in the day.

All the people came to comfort him. Fatima is sad, as she sat close to the boy in his bedroom. Now that there were signs that the boy was becoming lively again, everyone was looking happy.

The prayers were a continuing thing on a daily routine by everyone. No one knows who is praying what. There were no prayer points, only that which they started with to pray for the boy's safety.

All the people of the village had gathered, it appears that all the town were there. Everyone came to see what they can do to help. Most likely to hear once more about the proclamation that was made of the name 'AGIBU.'

The Chief had the leader Pa Karim read the words of the old woman, once again which was written in their book of truth.

So, Pa Karim read the proclamation, according to the word that was written in the book of truth. It was like a dream, so they took it lightly, and did not realise that it was an actual happening, decades ago.

After reading the words, he said, who has anything to say, let them say it. there was a deafening silence for a minute. Then the people who were gathered said, 'may the chief be praised.'

Not one of them want to say anything, so as not to provoke the chief to anger.

So, the people of the village kept quiet.

The people asked, 'what have they done to the boy?'

Both Pa Amadu and Fatima replied together, 'nothing.' All the people sighed and responded, 'we have never seen or witnessed anything like this before.'

The chief got up and went into his room to be alone with his 'god' to ask for favour.

But the group of people kept on praying. They stayed the entire day. food was prepared and served, and so were the drinks for the people.

It was a type of succour, for the family. They succoured all day and night as they continued in their prayers.

Agibu himself did not believe in tradition so he brushes aside his father's plea, about being careful what he does, `and the phrase, such as, 'watching after his back.' This was how it was told to him.

During the gathering everyone prayed. They offered sacrifices, they did rituals, and more of their cultural and traditional things. They offered sheep, goat, and chicken for sacrifice to break the curse.

During the gathering everyone prayed. They offered sacrifices, they did rituals, and more of their cultural, and traditional things. The offered sheep and chicken for sacrifice. But that did not do good to the suffering boy. His mind was troubled one way or the other; to believe or not to believe the tale.

After the gathering, everybody left as they came in, and so they went home in a solemn manner. There were intercessors who kept praying that all will go well in the house of Pa Amadu.

They all went to their various homes hoping all will be well.

Both Pa Amadu and Fatima replied together, 'nothing is going to help right now.' All the people sighed and responded, 'we have never seen anything like this before.' And they left quietly.

Chapter 3

The Curse goes on

Agibu incognito

After all the people who prayed for him had left, there were signs that Agibu was beginning to become himself again. He went incognito. He stopped using his first name. He now goes by the title

68

Prince as his first name and not as his royal title to disguise himself. Slowly he started going about his daily activities. He was definitely a smart guy.

'Superstition was not my way of life, and I would never be part of it,' Agibu thought.

The usual beliefs, and the traditions were not favoured by Agibu, so he distant himself from them.

He sometimes, wonders what all the fuss was about. Though he was upset, and had cried when he was told the truth, he still had hopes that things would change for him. That somehow, miracle would happen, and things will be normal for him again.

There were times when he thought about what had happened to his family.

'I wonder if my parents have gone out of their senses, with all the fuss they are making about me.' Agibu said allowed.

He could not understand why his parents where so paranoid, over-protective, and fussy about him taking up law as a profession. But knowing the story made him realise what the fear was. So, he called his father; and spoke to him that all these nonsense must stop. He does not want to hear anything about it again neither did he want to be part of their shallow thinking in the mind of all the people.

After Prince Agibu was born, Fatima did not have any more children. He was her only child. She was over-protective towards the prince. Even Prince Agibu was finding it difficult to comprehend. Little did he realised, that he was entering a dangerous zone. Would it be the wrong profession, perhaps?

A profession that requires him to mix with so many people from all sections of the community, as well as all works of life. Unknowingly that this would bring about the fulfilment of the 'Curse' and his early death.

A profession that carries hatred from most people who walk in dark paths. At the time when Agibu was about to celebrate his twenty-ninth birthday, his father was to celebrate his Seventy-two, and his mother her Sixty-ninth birthday too. Everyone was walking on tenterhooks.

Pa Amadu and Fatima had tried to conceive but were not able to. They were constantly trusting their 'god' to help them, and to bring them the son, which would be heir to the Chiefdom.

Only one creator which is the true God did it; and blessed them. However, they thought it was their idol in their prayer room that helped them. There were so many images that were in the room, that they kept sacred for their prayers.

They were all of varied sizes.

They were both past their mid age when they conceived their son. He was a late birth, considering the present day and the conception rate by the young people.

Judging from the fact that people have babies in their teens or before they could stand with their feet firmly on the ground, as people always say, meaning to be living independently.

Prince Agibu's father did not want him to work. Clearly there was no need for him to work. They were very, very, rich family.

Now that the prince had spoken to his father, it was time for the father to speak to him about settling down and marry. So, there were plans on the way to carry this pledge for a young woman. There was much to contend with, and the chief hired security for the young prince.

The child received daily monitoring. However, for life experiences, social interactions, and lifetime skills, his father let him. He had enough money to live on for the rest of his entire life. So, working was not a priority for the father.

The boy did not care about the family wealth. The prince is a dutiful young man. He helped with the regal duties. He accompanies his father to places to perform official duties. However, his heart was not in royalty. As he grew older, the family were thinking of marrying him off sooner, so, the plans were on the way. There were fair maidens to choose from. But their culture demand very rigorous planning and selecting of a woman for a prince, and this was on the way.

All the planning for choosing a wife for the young prince were on the way. In that culture, though the family will be involved, it would be the prince that would choose through a usual parade of young girls who have been groomed very well to be fit for a Prince. The young girls were ready for inspection by the prince and the family. There was going to be another huge celebration. Something like a beauty pageant show.

Specifically arranged for the prince, and family by the keeper at the women's house, so that they can choose their bride-to-be.

The Curse Goes On

Chapter 4

The Wedding: A Day with the Prince

The usual thing with the villagers were to have a ceremony to choose a bride for the prince. Fatima and husband not wanting to delay the process of finding a wife for their son; set about arranging for the well-groomed wife for the prince, quickly. So, they set up a meeting.

The Chief had started the procedure. In the town, there is a house of training where women go through the process of cultural grooming to be future wives, or

Princesses. This could last for few years. The sooner they get a suitor the less likely they would stay longer. In the house they would also be looking for suitable husbands for the girls. Those who stayed in the training school are those that can afford to pay for their grooming education.

The training which would include, Royal duties and behaviour, Etiquettes, Home duties, dealing with staff – such as house cleaners and servants. Also, taught were Community duties, motherhood, social duties.

The maidens were beautiful. They gathered together in one house in a huge compound, where there is an out-

building such as for the purification by the house keepers, for the chiefs' girls in the palace. A Chief can have as many as five wives. They would only choose girls that the keeper feels would be suitable for the Royals, and the rest would stay in the big training house.

Each of the girls that are chosen would have their own quarters, with house cleaner, lady in waiting and a servant. All of these people are staff, who are in training too with the girls. The women would have stayed for over twelve months in training, as they go through this elaborate rigorous preparation for womanhood.

The Selection Preparation

They chose the most expensive Oils with nourishments, which when made carries sweet smelling odour. When this oil is applied the girl's skin became smooth. and with a shiny glow.

Other things for beautifying the women, are things such as:

Beads for the body, were the best that could be provided. The women should wear the beads around the neck and waist area.

Head dress, and a skirt embellished with gold and silver trimmings.

Body adornment. Such as jewellery for the ears, neck and both wrists.

When the women are well adorned the time is right for the parade in front of the prince and his family. The chief wanted this arranged quickly so that he could have a second heir to the chiefdom.

When they should be time for the women to visit the prince, they were to be adorned to enable him to choose the woman who would be his wife. The women would be given all that they required to adorn themselves as described earlier. Everything would be given to them that they will need to function; if they are chosen to see the prince, and present themselves preciously in his presence. The fairest that is ready, (beautiful girl) would be given the opportunity to be prepared to attend the presentation. This young Prince who had wanted to give everything up has now bounced back into reality of life, and has dealt with the problem that shook him to the core. He is now preparing to take a wife. In fact, he was more delighted than Pa Amadu and Ma Fatima. He looked back at the journey from where he was, to where he arrived at now. His father was his mentor, and has been preparing him for the day he would become the heir. So, teaching a boy how to become a man is important to him and his family. When the Prince was a young boy he asked his father, 'why are you taking me everywhere?' His father would explain that he wanted him to learn the job.

The Process of choosing a Bride

There is a routine for every maiden. They have to walk past the prince and family few times. They would have to perform learned dance routines, and other demonstration. It is a show, a bit like a beauty contest. The girls have to show their beautiful body, not only their faces. The way they walk and move their body, their eyes are all part of the show. In these performances there would be different attire worn by the girls. The first would be half clothed (skirt). This means, from their shoulder to their navel is left exposed, but adorned with jewellery.

There would be three changes of clothes, The first attire is with the beads round their waist on top of a short mini skirt, which is adorned and embellished with silver and gold trimmings, this would be the choice of the prince's parents. The second would be an African attire of the prince's choice; and the last one would be an evening gown; this would be the girl's choice. These ebony beauties have body that glows, such like a glow that almost shines like a diamond. When they walk past the prince, he has to choose five from the twenty girls. Local musicians would be in attendance. Rumba drums

and Sambas are played by the group of
musicians who attends ceremonies. The
leader, Master Foday, directs the group
and they also came with their own
dancers. The musicians played in turns
to entertain the guests. There are also
conventional, and contemporary music
with their own MCs (master of
ceremony) musicians, each entertainer
has their own slot to play.

The Prince's Choice

Amira's natural beauty is a joy forever.
She is a woman of great physical
beauty, and of excellent quality. Well,
as anyone can see, she has attributes to
her beauty. The way she moves her

body, her graceful attitude towards womanhood, and especially her willingness to accept change of culture in her life, and not excluding her joy to want to accept the prince's hand in suit of marriage, if chosen, are all what makes up the attributes of her beauty.

The chosen five. The others have to return to their quarters. The five will spend the evening one at a time with the prince. Nothing intimate would happen. There would be people in the compound going about enjoying this party.

There are people who would be eating and drinking while all this parade is going on. It is an elaborate celebration.

Eating and drinking go on for two weeks.

This is called, 'An evening with the prince.' They both are going to get to know each other. Each of them would spend at least two hours with the prince, talking and doing activities.

After this first meeting, the five girls would then be released to go to their quarters. They would then have to visit the prince one day at a time. This would take a week.

Each girl would have to spend a day with the prince. It is from there the prince would choose who he wants to marry. This time, his parents would not be able to help him. It would be his own choice.

They had a Princess

Now, a week has gone bye, and the prince had got to spend time with the brides-to-be, and it is now time for him to reveal the woman of his choice. He was so happy and would laugh with an infectious laughter, and people loved that. The excitement was amazing. The prince has chosen a wife.

Things will now change that the prince has chosen a wife. We have a Bride. So, the message was sent to the Chief, and the preparation made for the announcement to be out. When the message is sent to the Chief, he would then make an order to announce to the people and public, revealing who was chosen to be the bride.

There has to be an announcement from the Prince's Office, managed by his father. We have a Bride. Said the notice.

So, the message was sent to the Chief, who would then make an order to announce to the people revealing who the bride is. Meanwhile, the guests were all ready to welcome the new Princess. So, Amira was the chosen one.

An African marriage has various ceremonial tradition that has to be followed.

Choosing a wife in an African tradition has great deal of planning, and ceremonial preparations, according to the cultural background of both the Bride and Groom. Even though the marriage was a royal affair, there still needs to be cultural input with all the parties involved. In this case, the Chief is the big spender to provide everything. The budget is limitless. The bride's family are ecstatic, and they are planning this wedding according to the wishes of the Chief who is footing all of the bills.

The Culture Shock

Their culture presents the glory of grace, and beauty of womanhood that cannot be found in any place more devoted to God's elegant design, such as in Africa.

And we can put this down to the creative designer, who is God, because of His love, strength, and vision for women.

An African marriage has ceremonial traditions, which has to be followed. It is right, so that the right woman is chosen. Marriage is a contract, and a lifetime commitment. If you get it wrong the first time, it is hardly ever it could be made right. This could render any woman a reject, if the marriage failed, and even if it is not her fault. Therefore, the home is where all begins, and taken up by the community at large.

So, the elders would take fine care of the choice that they support for their children. The children had respect for elders in the community. According to their custom the children should keep themselves from men or from having sexual relationship before marriage. In a true word, the men are looking for virgins. The girls are all eager to be virgins, so that they could be married to high class men.

Xsindolo Nkachi was the favourite of the women. She was one girl who had kept her womanhood intact. She went into the house to become the Princess. Before she went in, she was an independent woman who owned her own clothing business. She had been brought up not to engage in sexual activity. Girls are brought up to uphold there custom strongly by women who they call mama. When girls reached their adulthood, they are celebrated. Xsindolo had kept herself whole, and when she turned twenty-five. She was examined to be certified for marriage. On her being certified her parents sent her to the grooming house, to be eligible for the prince's suitor's parade.

But before she was sent there, her parents celebrated her for preserving her womanhood until her wedding, and not having children until she is fully ready to become a fully grown woman. She became successful in her business. Before she left, she said to her parents. 'Papa, Mama how do you know that I would be chosen?' They replied: 'you are the most beautiful woman amongst the maidens. So go and show yourself, our daughter.'

Xsindolo was one of the few who had degree in Business management.

Xsindolo was one of the fortunate girls to go into the house. Before she left, her parents celebrated her with a huge party. The physical piece of acceptance of her celebration is evidence that she wanted this change, and was ready for marriage.

In a way, one has to like and admire this part of the culture, the process of preparation, and the journey through to womanhood. I admit that it is there for us as leaders, and community to embrace it so it would work perfectly for us, and for our children, and for the love of everyone. As community, people should feed the children with all things good.

Womanhood

When the girls reached womanhood, they are eligible, and ready for marriage; then the cultural celebration preparation would be held to celebrate them. The girls are embracing the change of season that has arrived in their lives. Especially other young girls who were chosen in the parade too, have celebrated their womanhood before. As they were chosen to be in the house. Including Phebean Nmacula, Monday Karimu, and Sousu Makala. Picture the celebration of the women's accepting, and enjoying the celebration of Nzonda Nkoma who embraces her beauty with pride. It is spectacular.

This was every young girl's dreams of this day to come, and would seriously look forward to seeing the day that they would be celebrated. They all want to show off their ebony beauty. Their parents are celebrated as well for helping their children get to that point.

While this is perfect parenting, not everyone is able to tutor their children about womanhood. The children prefer outside help. Such as moderators who they will speak to, regarding puberty.

The value of womanhood

A community of mothers. These are women helping to manage, and strengthened young girls for their future home. Also, if there is trouble with them at home with their parents, that person will be the go between; or advocate to help quell the situation. At least, such moderators are seen to be playing positive role in society to the children; and to the parents. So, the saying goes, 'it takes a village to raise a child.'

The elders, and national culture is helping to avoid illegitimate children. Custom is the great force within culture that is, it works if no one is getting abused.

Looking into the African traditions; and culture is interesting in many ways. Those who have not got the opportunity to marry a Prince, or a wealthy man are married to men in a cultural customary marriage. Let us see what they do in this marriage.

There is a system that allows for men to put 'kola' to the women's parents, this is called the dowry. They tie things in calabash and includes all what a woman would need whilst going to the man's home. The downside is, in case the woman no longer wants to be married to the man anymore, the woman's parents have to return the dowry to the man. That was a known practice. I have never understood why this culture exist. But when a woman is married into riches there is no need to be asking for the dowry back. If they do, it is just a matter of revenge, or out of spite, as the women's parents cannot return the dowry because of poverty. For this reason, parents would work hard at their children's marriage to make sure it works.

I can suspect women suffered domestic violence because they cannot leave. This attitude is abusive, and it is awful. In my view, Customary marriages have led to the abuse of women in society. All this is got to do with money, and poverty, and not culture. Suddenly, women would lose control of managing the situation. Strong modern women would sometimes resist the temptation to stay in a loveless marriage, and risk the parents refunding the dowry. So, this is where we are at with customary traditional marriages.

Talking about wedding, in the chief's house, there is sharing; and they are super rich. The chosen Bride would have to be super healthy, and well groomed, so that there would be no fault. As explained earlier that maidens are well groomed by moderators, women who are elders standing for the truth, in place of parents for young women. These women elders know what it takes to be a woman, and above all the most important thing is so they keep their womanhood, in which checks would be made. They would have chosen the best of the best of girls from a virgin group of young women. So, they have to get it right; and the spending will be coming from the Chief for his only son.

'We have to take special care of the young women, report one elder. As for me, the women that are in my care, I always take fine care of them. When once a choice is made, I have to make it possible to give them that support, for their children.' 'Besides this wedding has a lot of money going into the preparation, which takes up to two weeks until the wedding day.' The best is what the suitors will do to let it work.

The timeline from the prince's selection day to the actual wedding day is seven days. In total, the celebration takes fourteen days of elaborate preparation, cooking, and partying. Then all will be quiet to leave the wedded couple alone to enjoy their marriage and bond. This will be their honeymoon period. Now that the prince had chosen his bride, let the celebration begin.

The Wedding Celebration

The officials at the house of Pa Amadu the chief, has planned a wedding celebration for the Chief. It is going to be one of a kind of all the parties the Chief had hosted.

The son, Prince Agibu will be married. He has finally chosen a wife, and is getting married. This girl is lucky. She is not from the same tribe as the Chief. Her background is from a very humble and poor home. Her parents can barely find food to feed everyone in her household. However, the family had saved up to celebrate her womanhood, and to get her to the house for grooming. Unlike the prince who is an only son, and has everything he needs. His chosen wife came from a family of six siblings, including her. Two mothers. The African marriage accepts up to five wives. This Princess-to-be came from the first wife of her father Pa Alieu. She was chosen, and now her family are going to be blessed through her. They are all happy that she will be settled in a lovely home.

Xsindolo was not chosen. 'How do you feel Xsindolo, that you were not chosen?' asked the reporter. She only had two words to say: 'next time' before she was swiftly ushered away back to the women's house. If ever she was upset, that was not visible in her face. This shows the integrity of a woman who had been managed carefully.

Whilst the engagement party was happening at the Chiefs compound, party was supposed to be going on at the women's house to celebrate all the other women together, so no one would be left out.

The Chief's son, Prince Agibu had finally chosen a wife, and is getting married. The announcement goes.

There was an elaborate party going on in the chief's compound; and you guessed it. There was also a matching party going on in the female quarters where the women were staying. There are no losers in the women's world. Every woman is a winner. Their beauty is their fortune. They all have the appearance that draws attention to anyone who sees them, and when they talk, heads rolled. Above all the women feel good about themselves; and why should they not? They have a creative design beauty by the divine creator.

The news came in, that the prince had chosen his bride. There was jubilation in the Chief's house and all around his compound.

This jubilation was that of happiness, and dancing all around the quarters, this continues for a long while. The people who gathered would not go home. People slept on the floor on mats with velvet blankets provided by the Chief's house.

So, the news came in that the prince had chosen his bride. It is all good, and everyone was excited.

As was reported, everyone was in a satisfactory mood. Feelings of joy clouded any mournful feelings anyone would have been feeling. It was clear that the happiness was felt everywhere. Even around the towns and villages. People were dancing in the streets in jubilation, with their own 'Ashobi,' and this presents a right spectacle.

'If you know these Chiefs as well as I do, they are in the habit of hosting parties, and throwing big feasts for their Princes when they choose their wives. Many of the people in high places do the same, and Pa Amadu is no different from any of them.' Reported the local news.

The guests comprise of Kings, Princes, Chiefs, Princesses, and all the Nobles of society, and servants, and other grandies. They all came from everywhere to celebrate this big day.

There were dancing of happiness all the way, through till the day for the wedding. As people hear of the wedding, they kept coming in groups to settle at the gate of the Chief's compound. These are professional stalkers at celebration. A bit like Mr. Spider (Bra Anansie) who likes attending weddings without being invited (as told in folk tales).

'Anansie bra spider' used to be everywhere, in the garden sheds, the flowers, the plants on the fence, the bathroom, the cupboards, and into every corners of the home. They came to enjoy, and be part of the wedding of the prince and his bride.

All the people who have been invited officially, will assemble on the Chief's great compound for this honourable occasion.

There were high class chefs to prepare elaborate round the world dishes. There was going to be a banquet in the evening. It was a huge thing.

The best and best of anything to eat that the mind could think of, and such as the eyes could see, were there.

This type of celebration gives cause for the Nobles, and the well to dos to show off, and display their wealth, and riches.

We see all the men displaying their wealth on their royal gowns. The same goes to the wives, and young women too.

This celebration goes on for seven days in the compound of the Chiefs huge acres of land. The location was perfect. The decoration reflects the lifestyle of the family, rich and famous.

All around were little Baffas, or coverings (tent like shelter), with coconut and palm kernel trees used to decorate the entire acres. Flowers were planted as if they were draped, and dressed, from top of the fence of the compound through to the ground.

The decorations are exquisite. It is such decoration that King's or Chief's celebrations are dressed in. Every elegant occasions are dressed in Purple and Gold. It was the colour chosen by the Chief.

After all the dressing, the place was looking more like a palm beach club rather than a Palace ground. Let us say at quick glance, one would imagine a botanical garden, with a touch of royalty, after all was done.

It was looking as if they had transported the whole botanic garden to their home. The family loves nature. It was green, so green, light, and inviting. There was nothing in the preparation that went amiss. It was lovely. There was an isle that the couple will dance down through to show off their joy of being married.

The guests were arriving. They were all served with Kola nuts, with a glass of mountain fresh spring water. This is the usual welcome by hosts to their guests on first arrival.

'Gifts should not be brought for the couple, but if you are moved; please donate it to the charity we have chosen,' said Fatima on the invitation.

Everyone came with a gift not for the married couple, nor the host family but for the family charity for the poor. The family had said, they do not want gifts. If the guests were moved enough, they were asked to give anything. It would be donated to their charity.

Guests came from everywhere, and from various villages, towns, and home communities. The guests were moved to bring homemade gifts, from their hometown, carvings, potteries, county cloths, even though they were asked not to.

Especially the kings, and Noble men who came with their servants bearing their own posh gifts of fresh herbs, spices, golden artifacts, and other special useful items for the home. People brought things from their farms. They brought Cattles such as sheep and goats. Also, chicken and duck. These means: the gifts were exhaustive.

The Ceremony

It was then time for the ceremony to begin; and everyone are now gathered to hear the pronouncing of the marriage between the prince and his chosen bride. First it was the traditional way, then they had to go the official way. But the whole wedding took place in the Chief's compound.

The wedding went on without any problems. Pa Amadu and Fatima were so excited. They were reeling with joy and happiness to see their only son eventually found a wife.

Prince Agibu was comfortable with his new bride Amira, and everybody just loved them.

See few of the African cultural arts that were donated to the family.

AFRICAN ARTS

The Party

Everyone was now ready to celebrate this beautiful wedding. Majority of the people have changed to their national outfits. It was elaborate. Everyone looked so gorgeous. There was a wedding party in which they danced, and enter the hall in twos. They formed a straight line in both opposite sides, with their dance partners, dancing through the isle, when they got to the top, they formed a line facing each other, leaving enough gap in the middle, so that the couple danced right through until they got to the middle of the dance floor. It is an amazing spectacle to watch.

Let me explain here what happens next. As it happens when the couple were on the floor dancing there was massive clapping, and displaying feelings of happiness for them. So, the couple are highlighting their style as they danced side-by-side into the hall, making grand entrance. So, the dance party now entering, it was a dance parade worth everything, and every money spent on the preparation. As was explained earlier, it was exciting to the end. Everyone had finished their dance routine. The Prince and Princess elegantly danced their way into the hall.

'Here comes the Prince and Princess,' they announced.

As a cultural thing, during their dancing everybody will start showering them with cash money. The husband would also shower his bride with cash from her head throughout her body. This couple makes money looks like paper;

everyone was throwing cash money on them whilst they dance. It is a majestic spectacle of celebration. It was grand. The colour scheme used which is purple explains the royal celebration. The elegance flows throughout the wedding party parade.

The prince is a good dancer, and there was a much-added elegance to the dancing, when the Princess showed off her dancing styles fit for the moment to rival her husband's moves.

As they approached the centre of the isle, the dance intensified. The Prince was now showering his Bride with cash money all over her. Money was flying around like paper. As everyone witnessed money shower galore as the groom, the family, and friends showered the bride with money.

At this celebration, everything was there. Even down to their most valued drink, the local produce of Palm Wine, was also there; and the people loved it. It is consumed better than any other drink because it is fresh, cool, and refreshing.

The alcohol in it was not that powerful. This batch they were drinking at the celebration was new wine. Freshly made and delivered for the wedding. It had not settled to mature into an alcoholic drink yet. So, it was fine for non-alcohol drinkers. The guests loved it.

You can say that there was abundance of the absolute best of wine in town for this royal feast. Everyone should eat, and drink to their heart's desire. The traditional loving cup was the star of the show. There was going to be this traditional loving cup drink. The people should drink from the chief's drinking goblets.

This should be passed round to share love and care. To the locals, it is a small calabash that the drink will be passed round with to share. For the rich and well to do it is a goblet.

A server would pass round with the drum containing the drink and another holding the loving cup ready to fill it when it is emptied.

This went down well, and the people loved the Chief even more for sharing his love.

When the wedding was over, the couple left for their honeymoon. When they returned home, they would now start living in the Chief's mansion. Now that the Chief had got his son married, he starts thinking of the heir to the Chiefdom.

The Legacy

It would be after Pa Amadu's death. He would leave him, as the only son, for that matter, part of the family wealth of millions of pounds. This wealth was built up from their family mining, and farming businesses. There was no other male issue to the family, from the other wives. After Agibu the Prince, the wives are the next to the Chief for any family legacy.

Pa Amadu had put money aside in a Trust Fund for Agibu, aside from the business. He wanted him to be independent, and not rely on state funding, or the business proceeds to care for his own family. He was oblivious of the situation, but since death is inevitable, he was forward thinking.

Prince Agibu had become a respected, and very independent hardworking young man in the community. He was always doing things to help others, and to help the family too. Prince Agibu is a trail blazer for young people. He is a pace setter, a bridge builder, and a leader in excellence, and loyalty. As he was thinking, he wanted to achieve the best qualification in the whole town, because they could afford to pay privately for his education. He had gone back to work after the wedding. He was a working royal as he does not want to depend on his family's assets. He loved his new bride, and always do anything to please her. Nevertheless, he knew of his fate but unknown to the Princess. This was a well-educated man. He had been doing fine in his work. Everyone was happy with him at his place of work, there were no visible enemy, and he made few friends. His manager had nothing to complain about, neither does he.

During his training, he took on his first case to work on, with an experienced Lawyer. Ironically, he prosecuted a young man who had attacked an elder woman in the street.

The Crown Prosecution Services was not aware of anything related to Agibu's family's problems. In fact, no one knew he was a Prince. He uses different name, and uses a different address from his family home. No one knew of the evil that surrounded the proclamation, and the story of the name bearing the Curse. But he was not using the name. It was a hidden fact that no one will know about. Only when names are to be chosen for a new-born child, people will know if there is good or bad attached to the name. The elders will look up the name, and will see the meaning in the book of truth.

As he was in disguise, no one ever knew who the real man is.

Chapter 5

Prince Agibu is Dead

Prince Agibu, (alias Korku) as prosecutor for the case. It was a short life. He had to go in to work on the day the sentencing was to be passed. He has the duty to be there to hear about the outcome.

On his way to the court, a young man stood at the entrance and said to him in a loud, clear voice, 'You know you are sentenced too?'

It was revealed that people heard him, and so was the security guard. Prince Agibu ignored the man, and went on to do his duty. How did that happen, that he got to where that threat was made? Even though he was going around with different name disguising who he was, no one knows. This is hard to understand. So, people were asking, 'Was it the name or his part in the case?'

He may not have heard him, or he heard, and chose to ignore the utterance. The young Barrister was coming out of the courtroom after the hearing, when out of nowhere came a mystery hand went straight for his chest. Nobody saw anything. All that people could hear, was the loud screams of Prince Agibu, and those around him. He dropped to the ground. He was bleeding heavily.

An unknown person stabbed Prince Agibu. He was attacked with a sharp blade that was thrust into his chest that very day. He screamed, and with a loud voice, then slumped down. He was badly hurt and was bleeding heavily. It was a sweltering day. People were tearing their shirts to stem the flow of blood, whilst awaiting the ambulance.

The sound echoed around the courthouse, and then there was a deafening silence, as people crowded around him.

The attacker fled the scene. He could not be found anywhere near the court. The people said, 'he melted.' He disappeared into the midst of the busy street. In the small town, people knew so many side streets and roads.

Prince Agibu was not from that town, and did not know how dangerous the place was. There were people around, but nobody could have envisaged what was about to happen on that day.

The ambulance came, and he was rushed to the nearest hospital, after trying to stem the flow of blood and resuscitate him, but he slept into coma.

The message was sent to the prince's parents, and his beloved wife Amira.

When the news came, Pa Amadu's soul was vexed within him. Nevertheless, the Chief got up, took the boy's photo, and placed it in front of their home idol 'god.' When he came out of his room, he summoned all the people who were at the naming ceremony to his home.

The Chiefs, the Imams, the Priests, the big people, the little people, rich, and the poor, everyone should show up. The town criers went to shout out to the people in the morning. Every small village in the town heard the calling.

Crying, 'Order, Order, Chief say, everybody should go to his home for an urgent meeting this evening.'

So, the people came in their numbers. They gathered. More than how they came when the baby Prince himself was being named. There were lots of people around. Those who were the masters, and mistresses of the ceremony.

Food were being prepared, drinks and snacks, and fruits, as it would be a long succour. Anything that you can think about in any huge occasion, was available.

They all came, and they gathered at the compound of the Chief. Everyone heard the news, as it was told by the Usher. They sang songs, they prayed; and they chanted. Others were crying, and were falling on the ground and rolling on the floor, yet nothing happened. They still have not heard anything from the hospital about the progress of the young Prince. Princess Amira was not able to contain herself, nevertheless, she had to go to the hospital to sit by her husband's bedside.

The Chief was sore. He came out of the prayer room where the 'gods' were kept, that he had bowed to. His face clearly shows that he did not get an answer.

Everyone thought their 'god' would respond to keep this young boy alive. No one wants to eat at first, though a huge feast was prepared because of the multitude of people who responded to the call.

Upon all these displays of passion their idol 'god' did nothing to keep the boy alive. Everyone was there from morning until night. Nothing happened. No one went to their respective homes. So, the people stayed, and succoured. There was plenty food to eat, and drink.

One elder took the kola nuts to get message, and performed the usual rituals when people are in crisis, so as to get answer. Still nothing happened. In the morning nothing happened. Then came night, and another day, yet nothing happened. The 'god' did not move. Pa Amadu was frustrated, angry, and cried, such as no one had ever seen of him before. Yet the boy laid down in the intensive care, silent as a rock. He thought to himself, how could name can have so much impact in so many people's lives? Pa Amadu asked the question silently to himself. Then he spoke aloud: 'Everyone should look out for names that can cause trouble in people's lives.' He concluded.

Pa Amadu's pain turned into anger very quickly. He could hardly contain his grief, as this incident changed him, and the community forever in a huge way.

As they were all there, the long-awaited news came, it was sad. The prince passed on to another world; and the prince slept. As the morning broke everything became clear.

The Curse Goes On

Chapter 6

The Prince Slept

Agibu's sudden death came too soon. The prince died three days after arrival at the hospital. The doctors and nurses tried; but there was nothing that they could do to save him. On that day, he was fatally stabbed, he should have been celebrating his twenty-ninth birthday.

Could he have been saved if he did not have a trial on that fatal day? I do not think anyone could have predicted the happenings leading to his death.

Though his father had thought that he stayed at home, to celebrate his birthday, the boy was doing the states duty. He had to attend. He insisted that it is his case.

When his father Pa Amadu received the call, he dropped down on the floor. He was having a heart attack. A massive pain was felt across his chest. So, he fainted.

Fatima stood over her husband as he slummed on one side grabbing his chest. Her mouth, her eyes, her face were all telling a story. The expression on her face was that of a broken person. She too was in shock, and of horror.

She sighed heavily, and then in a loud and clear creaming sound, then said, 'Now I believe in destiny O, I would have argued before all this, but now this is happening before my very eyes. It has happened to me, me, me Fatima.' She continued, 'now I realised that 'The Curse Goes On.' So, this is a Curse!' She sighed heavily as tears rolled down her eyes whilst the ambulance arrived to take her husband to the hospital.

Not long after the incidents, her house was filled with the usual busy bodies. More so, there were already people packed in the compound who were praying for the young Prince to be healed. Those who were there on the day the prince was born to Fatima and

Pa Amadu recalled the day of the ceremony. The traditional Naming ceremony. So, they remembered.

Fatima remembered the Elder, and the motion of expression on his face. The day the name was chosen, it all came back to her. Meanwhile, those around including doctors had made the Chief comfortable on the floor where he was sitting to wait for the vehicle to transport him to the hospital.

Fatima cried as she stooped over her husband whilst he was still lying on the floor, with tears streaming down her beautiful cheeks. She thought that was the end of him. He was taken to the hospital, whilst his son was in the morgue. The nearest family were in the hospital to support them. There were nurses and doctors. They were able to revive Pa Amadu. It was only when he came round, and was talking that the real identity of the prince was known. He spent couple of days in the hospital undergoing tests, and to recuperate. Then he was sent home. Amira also came home to wait and prepare for the funeral of her husband.

When Pa Amadu got back home, there was another meeting to organise funeral arrangements for their son, the prince.

And the Prince slept. He was buried a week after his death. No one who was present on the naming ceremony would forget the curse of the name Agibu.

The Mourning Ceremony

Those who came to mourn, came from all over. They were from various community faiths. The most prominent were the Christians, because they were differently dressed from everybody.

The Chief called his servants to remove the idols; and all what was in their prayer room, and bring outside to the fore court. He started bashing everything and breaking them to pieces. He was so vexed that he ordered the 'gods' idol to be burned. Everyone was standing speechless as they burned to ashes. Onlookers thought that he was extreme. But they do not know the extent to which he had been disappointed. That his 'god' has not helped at a time that he needed the help that was needed in his life.

How the people turned to God

Pa Amadu was so angry and spoke to all the people who are idolatrous. To do away with their idols. Idols does not do anything.

From the death of his son, he came to realise that the 'god' he was worshipping could not speak, could not act, or do anything to help him. So, he passed an order. The soldiers visited every homes to find where the idols were hidden. They were to bring everything that was found in the people's home, such things that they worship and bow down to, so that they may be burned.

Everyone who were at the chief's house were sent home to go and bring out their idols. They all went home, and started clearing their cupboards, and their rooms where the idols were centre stage. Everything was collected by the soldiers. Every single one of the idols were to be taken to the field, to the place where they were going to be destroyed.

However, the people were unhappy. This was the Chief's decision. But the

Chief quickly called for a meeting to pass a law for anyone thinking of defying the law, not to keep idols in their homes, neither in any of the religious centres were to be punished. The Chief made an order for the soldiers to visit all the centres, and the places where there are alters, and where people burned incense, and in worshipping the man-made idol. They set fire unto them, and they were destroyed.

That day it was a huge burn fire. After which tons of ashes were gathered. Buckets full of ashes were then taken to the river and disposed of. The town was purified out of the idolatry.

After all the excitement of the events that followed the marriage of the prince and his death, and the collapse of the Chief, things calm down for a while. Then the Chiefs of the town were gathered together once more in a meeting at the elder's court to make a decree. 'It has now been declared that the golden idols that sits in every home, has no power to heal or to save. That it cannot speak, and has no power to do anything to save their children's lives, so it must go,' said the head Chief.

They agreed that no one should keep any idol images whatsoever in their homes, nor burn incense to bow before it. Anyone found guilty of breaking the law would face prosecution, and if found guilty could face the death penalty, or the least an exceptionally long time of imprisonment.

Chapter 7

Changes that Bring Healing

As the time passes, people who came to wish the Chief well were from the Christian faith, and they had only worshiped the invisible God. They brought comfort, and peace to the family in the house of the chief and his wives.

The Christian group asked if the family would like prayers to which they agreed and asked. 'Which God do you serve?' and the people responded, 'The one creator of the world.' That is the God that answers prayers quickly. The chief responded, 'the people were corrupted, and thought that their idols would do anything they asked for.

I wanted to believe my parents who promoted their own way of worshipping, and so I continued. But I have never seen progression. If I had known your God earlier my son would not have died. From today, everyone in this village will worship your one true God.

We shall build a house for your God in every town where the people can go pray, and worship the God of all creation.

People of the village of course do not want to follow the decree. Few wanted to continue their abomination of sin to worship images. There were those who do not want to know, and they refused to attend the Christian prayer house. So, for a long time the church remains empty.

The chief asked the Christian people to share the word to the people. They were asked to visit the villages and speak to the villagers. They began to hold transformation meetings.

The disciples began to minister to them. They healed the sick, they provide food for the hungry, and build homes for the poor and destitute. Then the people began to have faith of the new religion.

One by one, and slowly they crept into the churches. Every Sunday, the house of God is pack full of hungry people for the word of God. All the people began to talk about this newfound religion.

When the chief visited the church in his own town, he urged the people to support their local church. To praise the one and only God. They were taught about the Bible, and to keep the commands.

The elders of the village announced that the leaders of the Christian church keep prayer meetings, and they began to pray for those possessed by evil spirts, and those that came to prophesy on the naming ceremony. Those with familiar spirits, idols, and images of their gods were prayed for, and asked that they cast them away so that the word of God can work on their lives.

The people were still holding on to their idolatry images, but after the priests prayed for them, they cast away their evil idols, and destroyed them. The people now turned to God, and started worshipping in the Church and keeping the faith.

Teachers were employed for the people. It was said that wickedness has increased, and the love of man had gone cold in that town. The chief went into his inner room and prayed to the Christian peoples' God to help with what he thought was abomination, and destruction of innocent lives, he would like the heart of the people to turn to kindness.

The news spread everywhere as people were being healed from long term ill health. People are taught to pray for one another. Then the biggest appreciation is when their farming became prosperous.

The Land became Prosperous

They have planted good seeds, and the crops are growing, the Lord sent rain, they have clean water, and their fields are watered, and everything started to prosper. Their soil was rich. Majority of the people now attend groups of church

Prayer meeting.

\#

WATER JUG

Key People

Pa Amadu Iscandor	Chief and Father of Agibu
Fatima Iscandor	Wife of Pa Amadu
Agibu Iscandor (Alias Korku)	The prince, son of Pa Amadu and Fatima
Isata Iscandor	Wife of Pa Amadu
Mariama Iscandor	Wife of Pa Amadu
Isabel Iscandor	Wife of Pa Amadu
Amira Iscandor	Wife of Prince Agibu
Pa Alieu	Amira's Father, The Prince's father-in-law
Madiu Sidique	Friend of the Prince
Pa Karim Koka	Elder of the Town
Kings, Nobles and Princes	The Rich Grandies in Society
Groups featured	People in the community
Phebean Nmacula, Sousu Makula, Monday Karimu,	Young Girls in the House

Nzonda Nkoma, Xsindolo Nkachi	
Christian Groups	Worshipers
Kola Nuts	African Fruit
Pottery	African Art

By default. A young Prince was living in disguise. But why?

Disillusioned by the name his parents decided to give him, he suffered the consequence. His death was a mystery. The death of this young prince brought about a change of healing in the sunny African community. A change by divine Solution in the community. It was a mystery and an end to the curse under sunny Dark Africa. It worked, and brought about the whole society together to destroy their 'gods,' and turned to the Divine Creator.

Did Pa Amadu get his heir? Watch out for II